DOCTOR
RABBIT

DOCTOR RABBIT

Story by JAN WAHL

Illustrated by PETER PARNALL

A SEYMOUR LAWRENCE BOOK / DELACORTE PRESS, NEW YORK

To Camille Barbara
from Uncle Mouse

The Rabbit was chosen
to be the doctor
because of all animals in the long forest
he was the quickest
on quick fur feet.

The first thing he did was
hang out a beautiful shingle—
RABBIT, M. D. it said
in pinecones and leaves.

Then
on the walls of the waiting room
he hung little poems
for the patients to read.

THE HALF-MOON'S SAILING ACROSS THE SKY,
THE WIND IS COMING, AND THE RAIN;
THE GRASS FEELS NICE AND COOL AND GREEN,
DON'T ASK WHY, DON'T ASK WHY.

Before he opened for business
he sat up late many dark nights
by lamplight
studying enormous books.

He asked all the old forest ladies
for their best remedies, then
tasted a spoonful of each of their medicines.

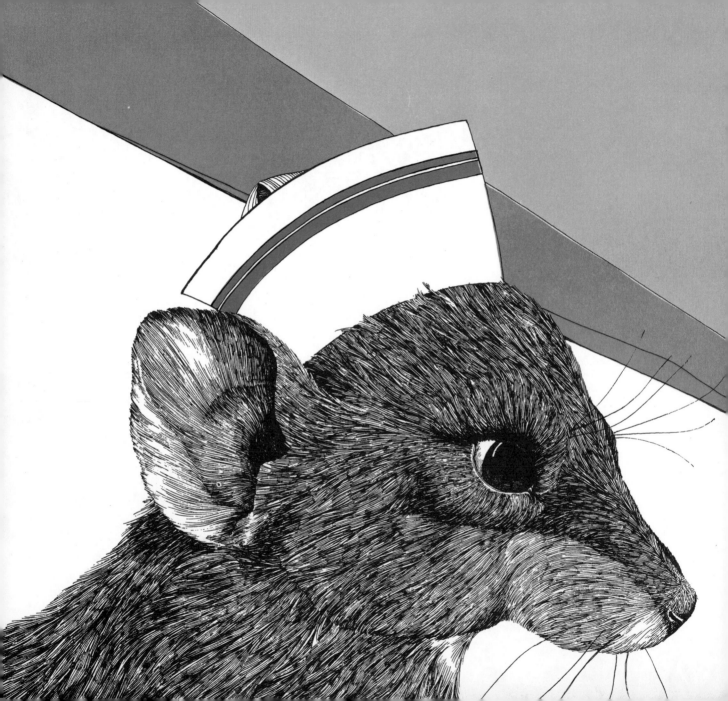

Miss Mouse
agreed to be the nurse.
She looked impressive in her nurse's cap.

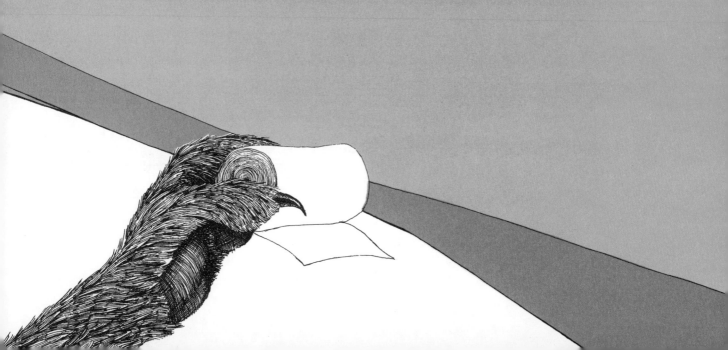

They practiced taking pulses
and giving artificial respiration
and listening to heartbeats
until they could do it
without a mistake.

After they had counted the pills
and everything was ready,
Miss Mouse rang a
little silver bell.

One by one they came
out of the bushes,
the holes in the ground,
and down from the trees,
the first patients.

They debated among themselves
who would go in first.
Miss Mouse solved that by having
them pick numbered acorns from a bowl.

The long-eared Owl
hobbled to the door
with a broken owl wing.
"I will make you a sling"
declared Doctor Rabbit.

The Badger and the Stoat
brought in a feverish cricket
on a leaf.
"Good grief" cried the good doctor.

The Raccoon's lip was swollen
from a yellow hornet's sting.
"You had better not sing"
advised the wise doctor.

The great Bear had gotten
pine splinters deep in his thick, padded paw.
"There ought to be a law"
sighed Doctor Rabbit.

The Squirrel had a sore throat.
"Don't go out now without a coat"
prescribed the doctor, writing it down.

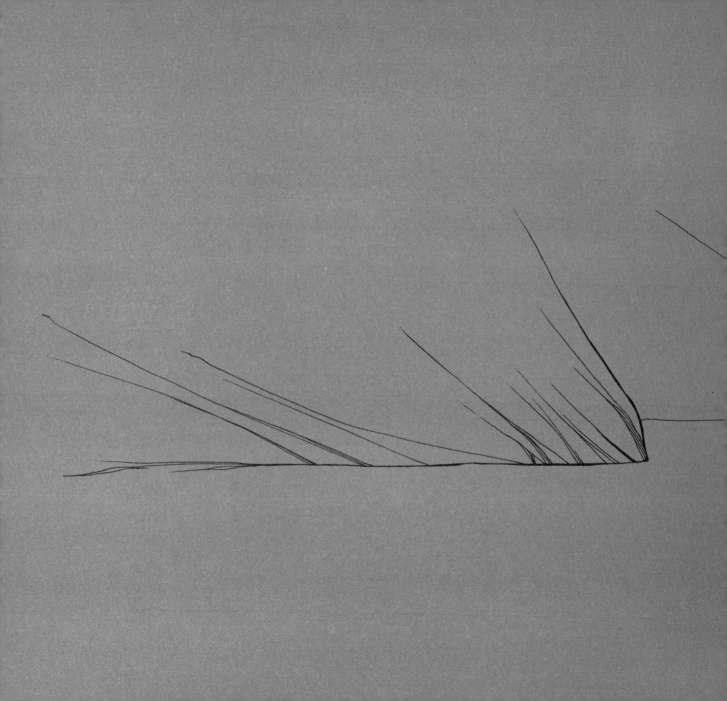

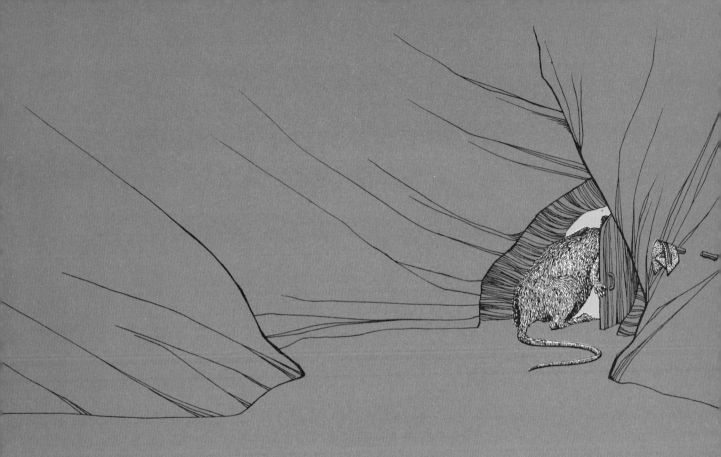

At the end of the day Miss Mouse
locked up and went home,
having hung her nurse's cap on a hickory peg.

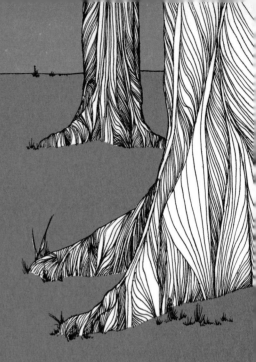

But at night Doctor Rabbit
would lie awake, worrying.
"If I fall asleep, a patient may
need me and I won't hear."
He sat up, concerned, thinking about that.

Outside the window grew a juniper
bush for smelling, and there
were twinkling stars in the
sky above to look at, yet what
did Doctor Rabbit do?
He listened. He listened. He listened.

Soon he heard Miss Mouse ringing
the silver bell. And the new day
would begin. He stiffly rose.
The waiting room was filled already.

Even when it snowed and
ice was covering every twig,
Doctor Rabbit bundled up and made
the rounds of his patients
faithfully.

Sometimes he was invited to stay
for tea. Miss Mouse always fixed sandwiches
which he carried, wrapped in wax paper,
in his doctor's kit.

When babies were going to be born
Doctor Rabbit raced through the forest
like lightning. Tired as he was!

However
one morning the doctor
was too exhausted to climb out of bed.
Miss Mouse put a sign on the door—
SORRY THE DOCTOR IS SICK.

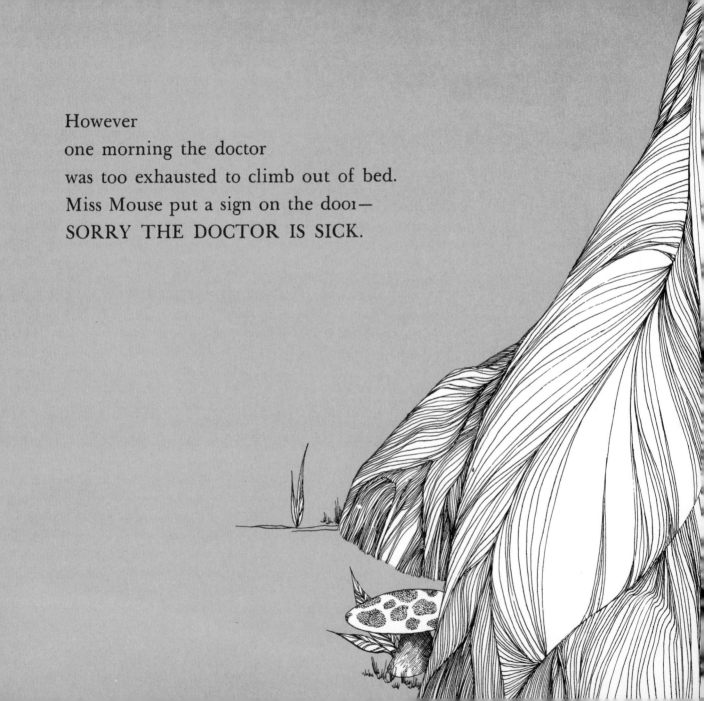

When the animals heard the news
they each brought one flower, a tiger
lily, a Columbine, a daisy, a red clover,
a shooting star.

They filled up the room with lovely flowers
and he sat in bed talking
to each of them in a very quiet voice.
"Don't talk, just rest," they told him—

and when he was sleeping and they knew
he really would soon get better,
they crept away on tiptoe, saying

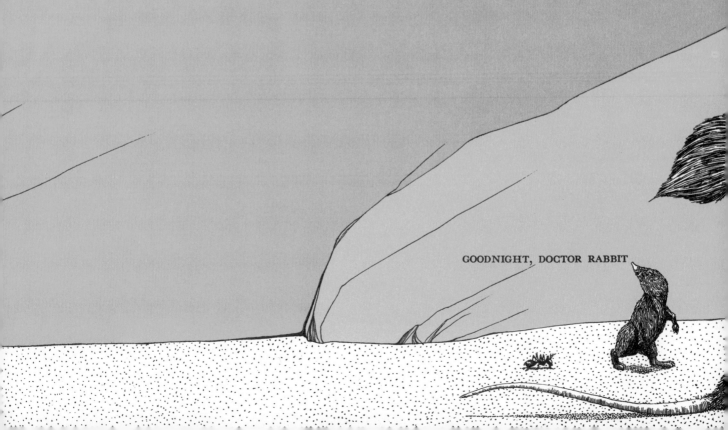

GOODNIGHT, DOCTOR RABBIT